Curious George

June 1998

This book is dedicated to my daughter
Ann Watness because she is happy
with who she is.   Watness, principal

VERDI

JANELL CANNON

HARCOURT BRACE & COMPANY

San Diego • New York • London

Special thanks to:

Clay Garrett, herpetologist at the Dallas Zoo for ten years
and editor of *Vivarium* magazine

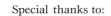

Robert Brock, senior keeper,
reptile exhibit, at the San Diego Zoo

Karen Weller-Watson, word surgeon

Requests for permission to make copies of any part of the work
should be mailed to: Permissions Department, Harcourt Brace & Company,
6277 Sea Harbor Drive, Orlando, Florida 32887-6777.

Library of Congress Cataloging-in-Publication Data
Cannon, Janell, 1957–
Verdi/[author and illustrator] Janell Cannon.
p.   cm.
Summary: A young python does not want to grow slow and boring like
the older snakes he sees in the tropical jungle where he lives.
ISBN 0-15-201028-9
[1. Pythons—Fiction.   2. Snakes—Fiction.   3. Old age—Fiction.]
I. Title.
PZ7.C1725Ve 1997
[E]—dc20   96-18442

First edition
E F D
Printed in Singapore

FOR MY STRIPED FRIENDS · RITA · BEN · MELISSA · IN · KALEN · AND FOR MY FELLOW HATCHLINGS · PAT · CATHY · BETH · WITH LOVE

ON A SMALL tropical island, the sun rose high above the steamy jungle. A mother python was sending her hatchlings out into the forest the way all mother pythons do. "Grow up big and green—as green as the trees' leaves," she called to her little yellow babies as they happily scattered among the trees.

But Verdi dawdled. He was proudly eyeing his bright yellow skin. He especially liked the bold stripes that zigzagged down his back. Why the hurry to grow up big and green? he wondered.

Maybe some of the older snakes in the jungle could tell him. Verdi ventured into the treetops to look for them.

Umbles, Aggie, and Ribbon were lazing on some branches nearby. Verdi peered at their droopy green bodies.

"It's not polite to stare," chided Aggie.

Umbles burped and groaned. "It's taken nearly four weeks for that last lizard to digest. I surely do like lizards, but lizards don't like me."

"Why don't lizards like you?" asked Verdi.

"Don't interrupt," Umbles grumbled.

"Dear me," whined Aggie. "If I don't shed soon, this itchy skin will drive me bananas."

Verdi tapped a tune with his tail as he waited to speak.

"Stop that, Verdi. It makes me nervous," Ribbon complained. "Besides, you'll never grow up to be properly green—always interrupting and constantly fidgeting."

Verdi couldn't imagine being in such a hurry to be like *them*. And he really wanted to keep his sporty stripes.

Hoping to find snakes that weren't so boring, Verdi slipped away.

Dozer was snoring in a tree not far from the others.

"Hello," said Verdi. "Do you want to climb trees with me?"

"I'm tired," Dozer growled. "Go do a few laps around the jungle, okay?"

Verdi's heart sank. Greens were not only lazy and boring, they were rude!

At the top of a very tall tree, Verdi gripped one branch with his tail and another with his little snake jaws. I will never be lazy, boring, or green! he thought. I will jump and climb and keep moving so fast that I will stay yellow and striped forever.

Then Verdi let go. . . .

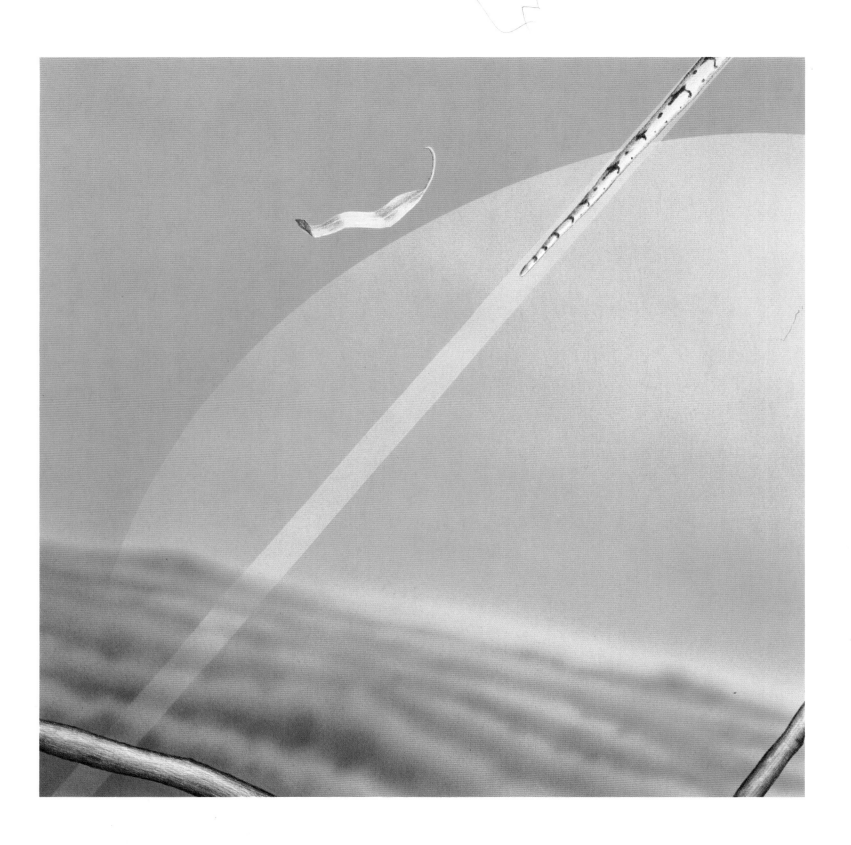

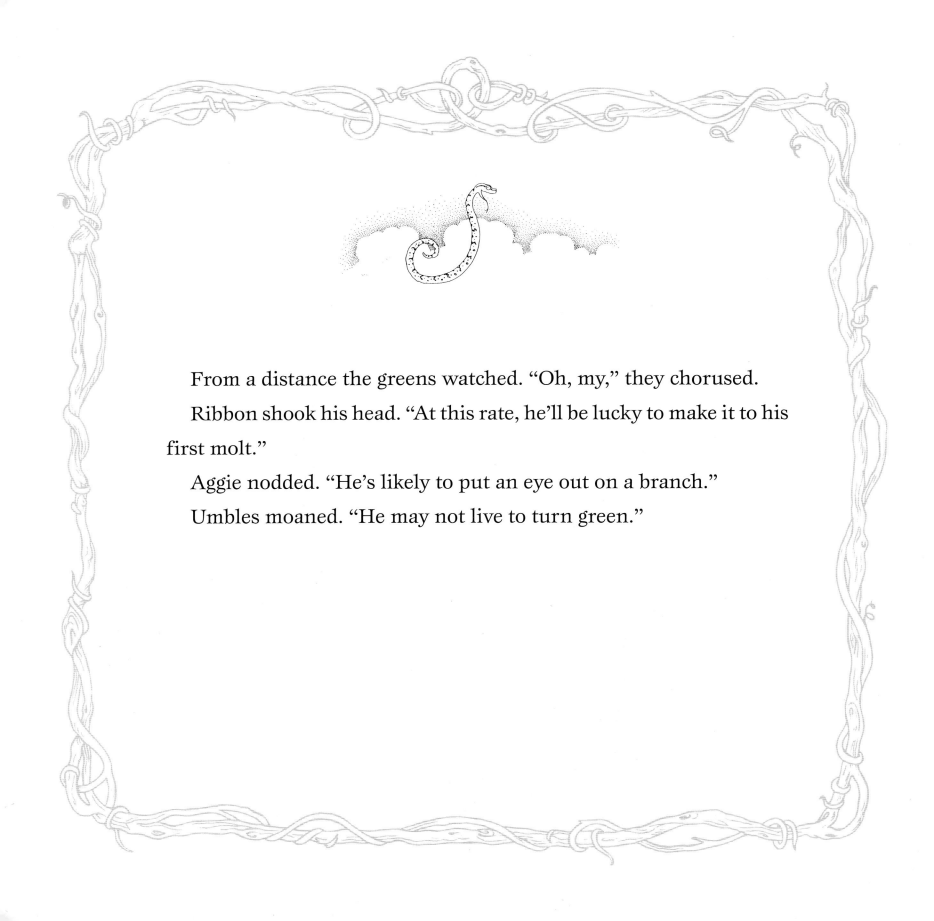

From a distance the greens watched. "Oh, my," they chorused.

Ribbon shook his head. "At this rate, he'll be lucky to make it to his first molt."

Aggie nodded. "He's likely to put an eye out on a branch."

Umbles moaned. "He may not live to turn green."

But one day, Verdi's skin began to peel, revealing a pale green stripe stretching along his whole body.

"KACK!" he gasped. "How can this be? I'm the speediest snake in the jungle and I'm *still* turning green." He raced down to the river, grabbing up a mouthful of rough leaves.

Verdi flung himself into the water. If I can't run this green off,
I'll scrub it off, he thought.

His frantic splashing caught the eye of a large bottomfeeder cruising the murky depths.

"Yummm," the old fish hummed. "Lunch!"

Before the fish could haul Verdi under, the frightened snake bit him on the nose.

Ah-POOH! With a blast of his rubbery lips, the great fish sneezed, sending Verdi into the air.

Slapping onto the soggy shore, Verdi skidded out of reach.

"Whew, that was close," he sputtered. Every inch of his body was covered with wet, gloppy mud. "Hmmm. Kind of lumpy. Kind of brown. It sure beats being green."

He left the mud on.

But the soft brown muck dried into a hard gray shell and Verdi could barely move. If he even budged, the stuff cracked off in jagged chunks. As each piece fell away, Verdi could see that his body was even greener than before.

"This is terrible!" cried Verdi. He pictured himself hanging around in droopy loops, itching and complaining and worrying all day like the old greens.

He looked up into the sky, where the sun blazed a beautiful yellow—just the color he used to be. Then he pulled a vine to the top of the tree.

Launching himself from the treetop, Verdi startled a flock of colorful birds. He became dizzy with delight, sure the bright sun and his lofty speed would turn him golden again.

In his joy, Verdi forgot he would fall back to earth.

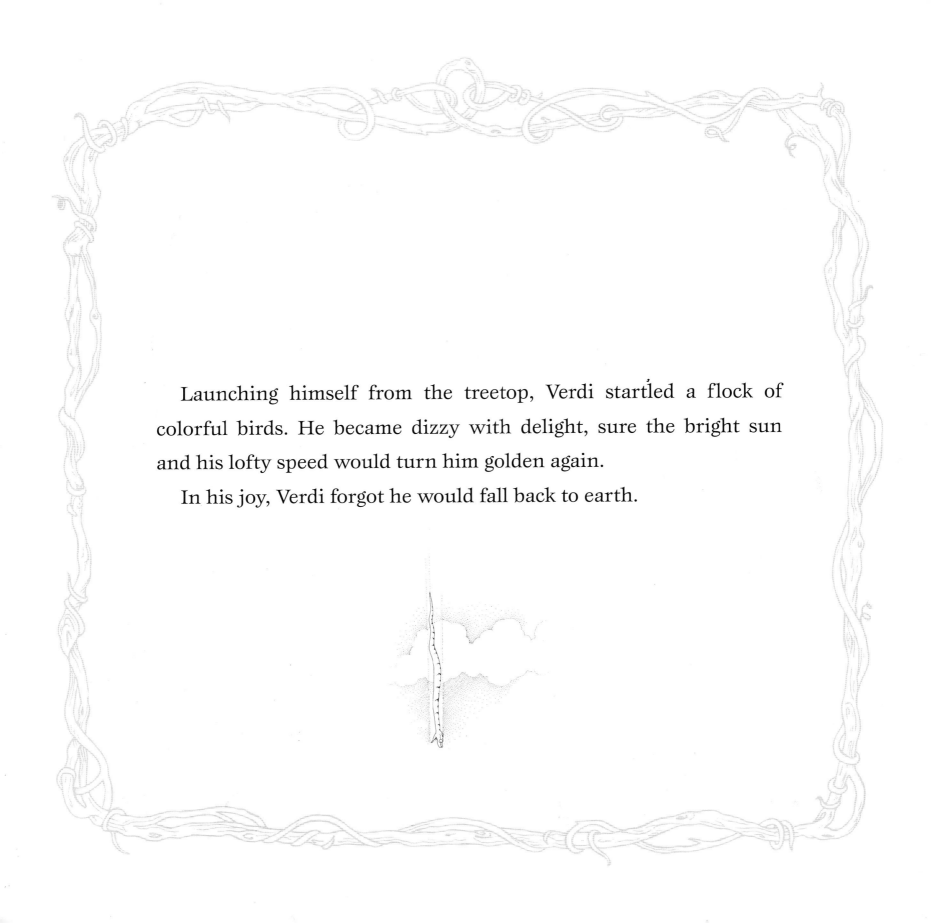

Whippety, whappity, fwip, fwap, WHAM! Plummeting through the trees, Verdi landed in a crooked sprawl across a log on the forest floor.

He couldn't move.

"Help," he croaked.

As usual, the greens had been watching Verdi's antics. They moved quickly to where he lay.

"Didn't we say it would come to this?" Umbles said, shaking his head.

Aggie sighed. "Lucky thing he's still got two good eyes."

They gently lifted Verdi up to a safer place, where they could watch over him while he healed.

Neatly splinted to a branch, Verdi had no choice but to listen to the greens as they gabbed.

"Remember how I used to streak across the forest floor?" Ribbon asked.

"Quick as lightning!" answered Aggie. "And I climbed giant trees like they were nothing. They grew taller then, you know."

"The things I dared to run down and swallow!" Umbles bragged. "Wild boar were no match for me."

Verdi was astonished. "*You* used to run, and climb, and hunt giant pigs? What happened?"

"Ribbon crashed—just like you," Aggie replied. "I took a terrible fall and almost put an eye out. Then old Umbles here nearly choked to death. Now we all prefer the quiet life. A warm perch, a little sunshine, and an occasional good meal."

The greens rambled on about their days of glory, and Verdi settled in on his branch.

Finally one afternoon, Umbles said, "Looks like you are ready to go again." He carefully untied Verdi from the branch.

"You are welcome to come with us," said Aggie.

Ribbon agreed.

The three greens slipped quietly back into the forest.

Verdi wasn't ready to join them. He wasn't sure where he wanted to go, so he just stretched and stayed put until the sun went down.

He listened to the forest come alive. . . .

Time passed. The sun and moon took turns in the sky. Verdi marveled as the full moon grew thinner every night. Then he watched patiently as it slowly grew round again. He wondered why he hadn't noticed that before.

Verdi became so green that he blended perfectly with the leaves. He was so still that other creatures walked right by without seeing him.

One fine morning as Verdi basked in the sunshine, two small yellow snakes approached. They tapped and fidgeted as they stared.

"Get a load of that old green guy," one of them whispered. "Do you think he ever moves?"

The other snickered. "I seriously doubt it."

They're just like I used to be, thought Verdi. And I'm now what I was afraid to be. He looked at his big green body and slowly smiled. "How would you like to climb trees with me?" he asked.

"With *you*?" The yellows were astounded.

"I'll even show you my fancy figure eight," Verdi replied, though he was a little worried about putting his eye out.

With practice the three snakes performed a perfect *triple* figure eight.

Leaping and looping with his little striped friends, Verdi laughed. "I may be big and very green, but I'm still me!"

SNAKE NOTES

THERE ARE ABOUT 2,500 species of snakes. From tiny thread snakes just 4 inches long to giant reticulated pythons that grow to nearly 33 feet, snake populations are native to all parts of the world, except Ireland, Iceland, New Zealand, and the polar regions.

A snake's skin is dry, not slimy as many people believe, and their scales are tough. Depending on the species of snake, scales may be shiny and smooth or very rough. Some snakes actually polish their scales by rubbing them with an oily secretion from a gland by their nose.

While many snakes see very well, others are blind. Most use their nostrils to pick up scents. Snakes use an inner ear, as well as other sensors in their bodies, to detect vibrations around them. Some snakes have heat-detecting pits in their faces that help them to hunt in darkness. All snakes rely on their delicate forked tongues. As the tongue darts out, it collects chemicals from everything it touches; when it withdraws, it passes over the vomeronasal organ in the roof of the snake's mouth. This organ processes the chemicals, providing the snake with important information about its environment.

Snakes are carnivores, which means they eat animals. Their diets can include insects, reptiles (even other snakes), fish, eggs, birds, and rodents. Some of the biggest snakes will eat creatures as large as a deer. Many kinds of snakes can go months without eating.

About 25 percent of the world's snakes are venomous. Their venom is used to quickly paralyze prey, and for self-defense. Although most snakes would rather flee than fight, it is smart to admire all wild snakes from a distance. These often-shy reptiles will appreciate your respect.

Among the many nonvenomous types of snake is the family of giant snakes, Boidae, which includes all pythons and boas. While boas are ovoviviparous, meaning they birth their babies fully formed, pythons are oviparous, which means they lay eggs. Green tree python *(Morelia viridis)* mothers protect their eggs until hatching time—nearly two months. Once they emerge, the baby snakes are on their own. These hatchlings range in color from dark reddish brown to bright yellow. Approximately 8 inches long when they hatch, these babies grow to about 6 feet. After several molts, their skin colors change to the rich green of a mature snake.

The young snakes eat insects and small lizards, using clever techniques to capture their food, such as wiggling the wormlike tips of their tails to lure their prey within striking range. Adults become adept at capturing birds by curling up and resting

motionless in trees before striking. Their unusual coiling position allows them to operate much like a 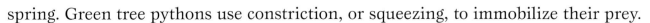 spring. Green tree pythons use constriction, or squeezing, to immobilize their prey.

Snakes are valued by humans for many reasons, including their ability to keep rodent populations in check. These sensitive creatures are an important part of our ecosystem.

The illustrations in this book were done in
Liquitex acrylics and Prismacolor pencils on bristol board.
The display type was hand-lettered by Judythe Sieck.
The text type was set in Esprit.
Color separations by Rainbow Graphics, Hong Kong
Printed and bound by Tien Wah Press, Singapore
This book was printed on totally chlorine-free
Nymolla Matte Art paper.
Production supervision by
Stanley Redfern and Ginger Boyer
Designed by Lisa Peters